W9-AZS-780

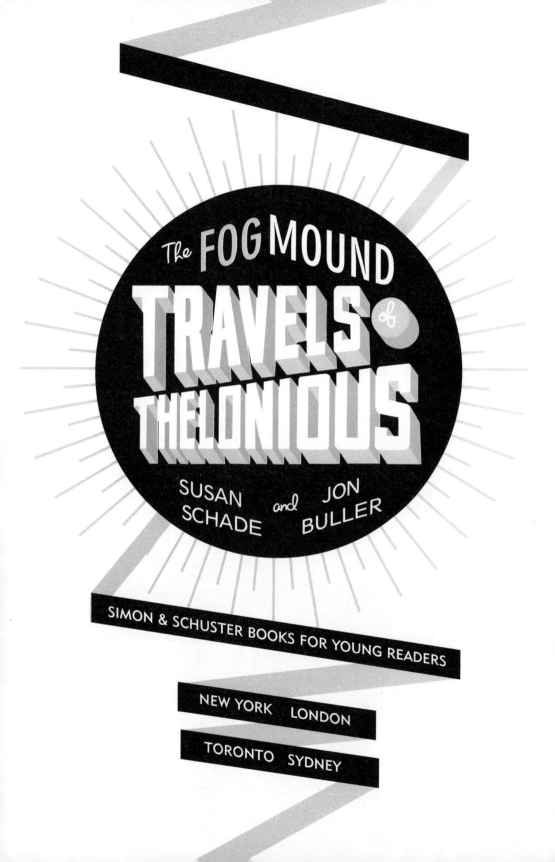

The Fog Mound

The **FOG MOUND**

TRAVELS *of* **THELONIOUS**

SUSAN SCHADE *and* JON BULLER

SIMON & SCHUSTER BOOKS FOR YOUNG READERS

NEW YORK   LONDON

TORONTO   SYDNEY

SIMON & SCHUSTER BOOKS FOR YOUNG READERS
An imprint of Simon & Schuster Children's Publishing Division
1230 Avenue of the Americas, New York, New York 10020
Copyright © 2006 by Susan Schade and Jon Buller
All rights reserved, including the right of reproduction in whole or in part in any form.
SIMON & SCHUSTER BOOKS FOR YOUNG READERS is a trademark of Simon & Schuster, Inc.
Book design by Daniel Roode
The text for this book is set in Geometr415 Lt BT.
Manufactured in the United States of America
2 4 6 8 10 9 7 5 3 1
CIP data for this book is available from the Library of Congress
ISBN-13: 978-0-689-87684-4
ISBN-10: 0-689-87684-X

FIRST
F
EDITION

For Jimmie, Essie, and Nerl

Thanks to John Warwick Boyd for permission to use his poem "Bwoo Bwoo."

Visit Susan Schade and Jon Buller at their website
www.bullersooz.com.

In ancient times, when human beings ruled the earth and the animals did not yet have the gift of language, there was born a certain human baby, and he was named Bob. . . .

That's how one of the old legends starts.

I have always liked the human beings in old legends, and Bob is one of my favorites. When he grows up, he saves some lab animals from a mad scientist.

But the first time I ever heard *The Story of Bob*, I wondered why the legend said that animals did not yet have the gift of language. How could we have talked to each other if we didn't have language?

I asked my mother what it meant, and she answered, "I think they mean the gift of language *as you and I are speaking it now*. They say that there weren't any truly talking animals during the Human Occupation, that all of the animals communicated only in the low language—you know, the grunts and growls and purrs and so on. In fact, that was what separated humans from animals."

"But then, how did we get the gift of language? Who gave it to us?"

"Oh, grow up, Thelonious!" said my sister, Dolores. "There are talking animals like us, and then there are the grunters and growlers. That's the way it is. The Human Occupation is just a myth, *The Story of Bob* is just a story, and human beings aren't real!"

"They are too!" I cried.

I was pretty young back then.

But even later—after I had my own house and my own nut pile—I still believed in the old legends, and in human beings, too.

And Dolores was still acting like an older sister. . . .

1

The Untamed Forest

5

6

7

8

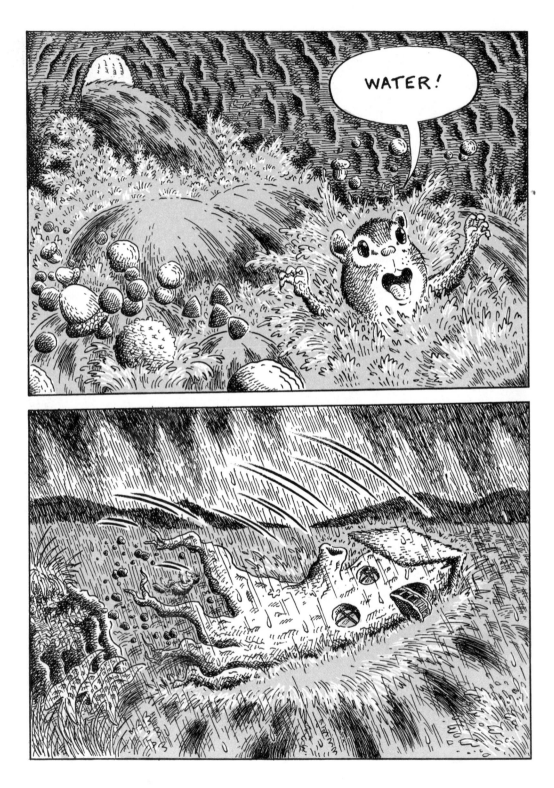

10

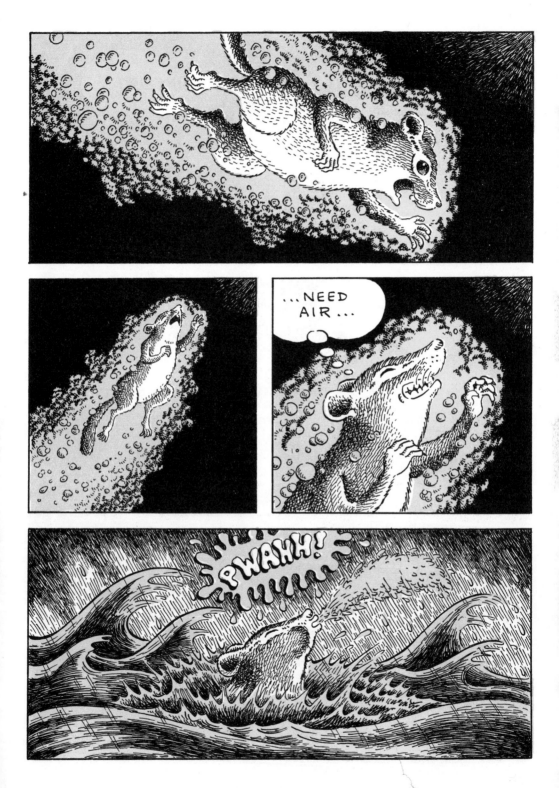

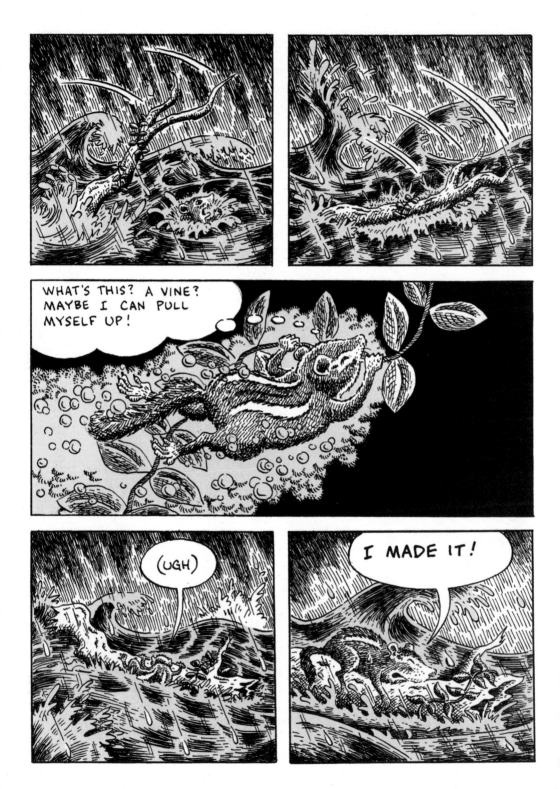

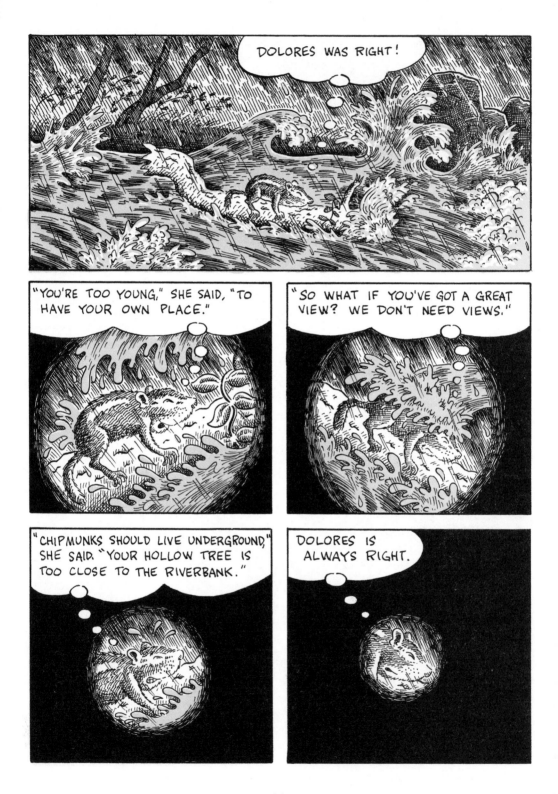

2

The Unknown Territory

I woke up slowly.

I could hear a little *lap, lap* sound of water on pebbles—that was all. The roar of wind and water had finally stopped. The storm was over.

I noticed a strange, sour smell in the air, and I opened my eyes.

I saw that my branch had come to rest close to the shore. Good.

But . . . *where was I ?*

A large figure came toward me, out of the mist.

I didn't move.

It came closer. And closer.

Now I could see that it was a bear. A big one. A bear wearing clothes! She bent down to pick something up.

Then she came closer still, examining the strange object. Luckily, she didn't see me.

I stared at her clothes.

In the Untamed Forest you might see a talking animal wearing a home-made rain hat, or a bright feather, or a necklace of nutshells. And my friends and I sometimes played make-believe, wearing capes of leaves. But I had never seen clothes like the ones on this bear. They looked like something a *human being* might have worn!

I could hear the bear humming to herself as she moved off and disappeared into the mist.

I waited for a few minutes, watching and listening.

Then I jumped off my branch and scooped up a drink of river water.

Gaaak! I spit it out. It tasted yucky! *Pah! Ptui!*

I tried sucking some of the rainwater off my branch instead, and I was relieved that it was okay. Then I waded through the bad-tasting water, up to the rocky shore.

Trotting over the pebbles, I said to myself, *When I get to the safety of the trees, I'll find a local chipmunk—someone who can give me temporary shelter and some food and show me the way to go home.*

I hurried along, watching out for bears. The mist had thinned out, but now the sky was growing dark. I hoped I would reach the tree line soon.

After a while I slowed down. I thought, *Where are all the trees?*

I stopped and looked around. My mouth felt dry, and there was a sick feeling in my stomach.

There *were* no trees!

And not only that! There wasn't even any grass, or *anything*! There was

nothing green. Nothing growing. Nothing alive. As far as the eye could see it was all hard and gray, with pointed rocks and high cliffs—cliffs that went perfectly straight up and down and were full of square holes.

It was all so . . . unnatural! I didn't like it. And besides, what was I supposed to eat?

I stared up at one of the cliffs. It seemed strangely familiar to me. I thought, *Where have I seen something like this before? Not in the Untamed Forest, that's for sure! It must have been in a dream.*

And then it came to me.

What I was looking at wasn't a cliff. It was a human building! I recognized it because I had seen a *picture* of one before—on my human artifact card!

Aha! I thought, and I touched the wall beside me. *This is real! It's a real human building. And that means humans were real! I was right! I knew it. Oh, boy, wait'll I tell Dolores about this!*

It was just that I hadn't expected human buildings to be so big. These were HUGE.

And that wasn't the only thing. The one on my card had been whole. These were falling down, and deserted, and . . . lonely.

"Hey, you! Kid!" someone called.

I jumped and whipped around. I had been forgetting to be watchful! (Most of the time I am very watchful.)

I didn't see anyone.

"Over here!" A clothed arm appeared through a crack and waved a glittering chain. "You wanna buy some real gold, kid?"

Somehow, I didn't trust that guy, even if he *was* a talker.

I said, "No, thanks," and I backed up.

"Buzz off, Weasel!" A talking lizard stepped out from behind a pile of broken stone and leaned against a rock. The arm with the dangling chain disappeared. To me, the lizard drawled, "You're new around here, aren't you?"

I looked at him suspiciously. I had never heard a talking lizard before. And *he* was wearing clothes, too—a black shirt, and a red cloth around his neck.

What's with all the clothes in this place, anyhow? I thought. *Does everybody wear them?*

"Don't worry," the lizard said, holding his hands out, palms up, and turning them over. "I'm not armed."

(And what did he mean by that? They looked like arms to me.)

He folded his arms (or whatever he wanted to call them) and looked me over.

"This isn't a very safe place for a little guy like you," he said. "Especially one who doesn't know the ropes."

"I'll be all right," I muttered.

The lizard snorted. "Yeah, right!"

He leaned against a wall. "You come from up north? Untamed Forest, maybe?"

"So what if I do?" I said.

He nodded. "Thought so," he said. "We don't see many chipmunks around here."

"What is this place, anyway?" I asked.

The lizard gave a short, nasty laugh. "Welcome to the City of Ruins, Chipmunk," he sneered.

The City of Ruins! No way!

The City of Ruins is one of the creepiest legends I know. I used to tell it at the Rock Cave sometimes, when the talking animals got together. It starts like this:

In the ancient City of Ruins, where the river mixes with the sea, where tall buildings still stand, and where the good earth remains buried to this day under a hard and lifeless crust . . .

I had told that legend many times, but I never thought it was about a *real place*!

Still, the ground here *was* "a hard and lifeless crust," all right. I scuffed against it with my foot. And there were "tall buildings" still standing. I looked up at them. Well, *some* of them were still standing.

"I said, 'Welcome to the City of Ruins,'" the lizard repeated. "You heard of it?"

I nodded.

He beckoned to me. "C'mon, walk with me," he said. "You'll be all right. I've got protection."

He held up the cloth that hung around his neck. "See this red scarf? It

means I'm under the protection of the Dragon Lady. Anybody who messes with me has got to answer to the Dragon Lady and her ratminks. If you wanna survive in this city, you've gotta have protection."

Protection from what, exactly? I wondered.

I thought about the words in the legend:

Hidden within the City's gates lie riches untold, and drawn to the riches, like moths to the moon, come stealing, come creeping, the most evil and ruthless criminals known to Animalkind . . .

Now I was scaring myself. I hurried to catch up to the lizard, and I walked beside him. But not too close.

I wondered if he had any food on him. And whether I should ask him about getting home.

"See, the City of Ruins has got a lot of criminal predators," he was explaining. "Snakes, owls—you name it, we've got it."

He looked from side to side. "It might seem quiet now, but that's because most of them come out later, when it's full dark.

"My protector, the Dragon Lady, she would like you," he continued as we walked. "She likes unusual animals, especially small, furry ones."

For some reason that made him laugh.

"She'll give you a good, safe job," he said, snickering. "Like washing floors, or something. It's your best bet. And you'll love the palace! Wait'll you see the jewels she's got! If she likes you, or if you do her a service, she might even give you one."

He rubbed his hands together. "I've already earned a few jewels myself—my two pearls, my diamond, my black opal, my moonstone."

He was walking faster now, and almost talking to himself. "There's that big ruby. She says the next time I do her a service, she might give it to me!"

He chuckled, then muttered, "Yeah. I'll bring her a nice chipmunk slave. She'll like that!"

I stopped.

"Bring her a nice chipmunk slave? I don't think so!"

And I turned and ran.

3

Underground

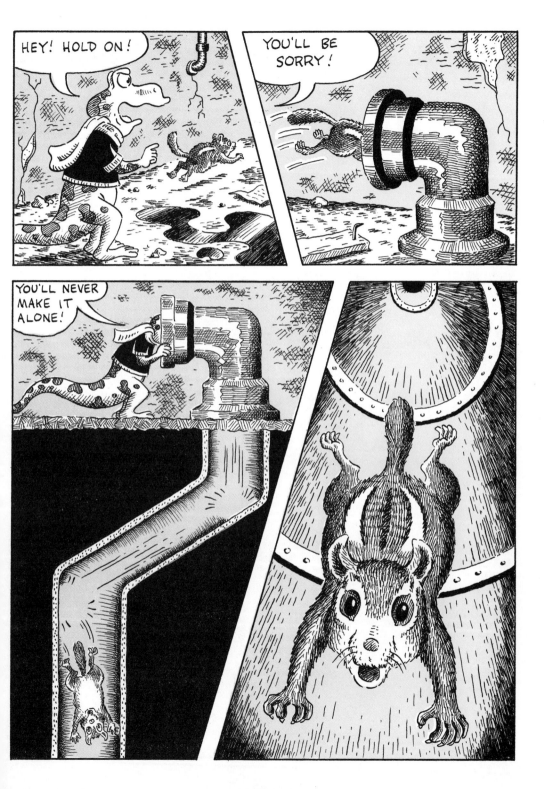

32

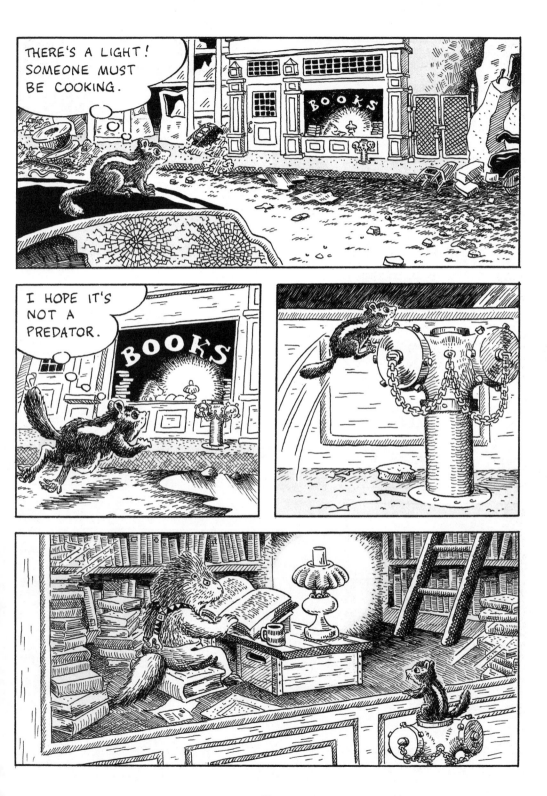

OOOH...ONE SIP!
IF I COULD ONLY
HAVE ONE SIP!

4

Fitzgerald

I was inside.

The old porcupine was standing over me, hands on his hips. He was wearing pants that were held up by straps, and there was a hole in the back where his tail stuck out.

I waited. I was all burned out. It had been a long day, and I was too tired to run anymore.

The porcupine reached for me.

I didn't flinch. I would take whatever was coming to me like a trouper.

He grunted in the universal low language that all animals, even grunters and growlers, can understand. The sounds meant, "Me, friend." (He was friendly! He just wanted to touch paws!)

I managed to place a limp paw in his big one and croak out the words, "Thelonious Chipmunk, Untamed Forest."

"A talker, huh?" He straightened up and stared at me. "And from the Untamed Forest! You surprise me. Are there many talkers up there in the Untamed Forest?" he asked.

I didn't know what he would call many.

I said, "When we have our All-Forest Meets, we get around thirty or forty talking animals, give or take a few."

"Any talking predators?" he asked.

I nodded. "There's a family of foxes," I said. "They've sworn not to eat other talkers, but I don't feel safe around them. I mean, suppose they get hungry?"

"Interesting," he said. "So how the heck did you . . . No," —he stopped and shook his big head—"never mind. We'll talk later. Right now, you look exhausted. And I'll bet you're starving, too. Wait here, I'll be right back. Oh, and by the way, my name is Fitzgerald. Pleased to meet you."

Fitzgerald shuffled out of the room, his rough tail swishing back and forth on the dusty floor.

I just sat there, breathing. I wasn't planning on going anywhere.

It was a big place, and it was full of books.

I knew about books. I had even seen one once.

It was back home in the Untamed Forest, on the traveling peddler's cart. The peddler had showed us some paper inside two hard covers. He claimed it was a human artifact, called a book, and that the words on the papers spelled out old legends.

Dolores hadn't believed him, but I had. I liked telling legends. I already knew the alphabet, and I could spell my own name. I could even sound out other words, if I had to, and scratch messages in the dirt like, "T. WUZ HEER," or "V. LUVZ GRLZ." But I didn't buy the book. The peddler wanted two baby rabbits for it, and we weren't supposed to be visiting him, anyway.

When Fitzgerald came back, he was carrying a perfectly smooth, round bowl the color of ripe blueberries. He set it down on a table and helped me up beside it. The bowl was full of juicy, golden peaches, peeled and sliced.

I took a big piece of peach and stuffed it in my mouth. The juice ran down my front.

I was beginning to feel better already.

After a few more bites I asked, "Where are the peach trees? Are they anywhere near here?"

"Peach trees?" He looked surprised.

I held up my piece of peach.

"Oh. *Peach* trees. Ha, ha! Boy, have you got a lot to learn, Chipmunk. Here, let me show you something."

Fitzgerald went out of the room again. This time he came back with a cylinder that had a beautiful colored picture on it.

He held it up and watched me to see what I thought.

The picture was almost as nice as my old card—or maybe even nicer.

It was of a peach tree with big, ripe peaches hanging from the branches. There were letters, too. S . . . U . . .

"Did you ever hear of canned food?" Fitzgerald asked me.

I tore my gaze away from the bright picture and looked into the porcupine's grizzled face. "Canned food?" I said. "Yeah, I've heard of it—in legends. They say the humans knew how to seal up food in cans, so it would last a long time, and they could eat it when they ran out of fresh."

I looked back at the picture. "You don't mean . . ." I pointed to it. "Is that . . . ?"

"That's right," said Fitzgerald. "This is a can, and there are peaches inside. You just ate some canned food. Not bad, huh?"

No way! I looked at my slice of peach. I smelled it. "This isn't *human* canned food," I said.

"Sure it is. What else would it be? Porcupine canned food? Ha, ha!" He laughed.

I said, "But . . . I mean . . . it must be pretty old!"

"Yeah, well, lucky for us the humans had really perfected the art of canning. Judging by what they did to the planet, I guess they needed to. This stuff lasts forever."

"What *did* they do to the planet?" I asked him. This was something I had often wondered about.

"Oh, well, as to that, I don't know *exactly*. Used it up, I guess. I haven't

found anything about their final days in any of my books. And I've got a lot of books." He gestured at the shelves around him.

I looked at the books again. I thought about who had made them, and what the words inside had to say.

"These are human books, aren't they?" I said slowly.

The porcupine was watching me. "Of course. This *is* a human city, Thelonious. Don't you even know where you are?"

"This lizard I met said it was the City of Ruins," I said.

I told him about the lizard.

"That sounds like one of the Dragon Lady's spies," he said. "I've heard of him. I think you were pretty smart to run away."

So then I told him about the rains and the flood, and my home in the Untamed Forest. And I told him about waking up where it smelled strange and the water tasted bad, and about the Bear in the Mist, and about the big underground tunnel.

"Is that human too?" I asked.

"Of course it's human. Trains used to run through it."

I had heard of trains. I tried to imagine a line of closed metal wagons

running through the big tunnel. And then I thought about all the other human things I had heard of—like motor cars and washing machines and mail, and computers and fireworks. *Were they real too?*

"So, yeah," Fitzgerald was saying. "This is a preserved human city. We even *live* on human relics. Nothing grows here, you know. If it weren't for the canned food in the stores, nobody but predators could survive. Luckily, the stores are filled with everything you could possibly want."

I thought about that. I was pretty sure "stores" didn't mean Fitzgerald's own storerooms in his home. It meant *public* storerooms where humans had traded money for goods. It was like going to the peddler's cart.

I said, "You mean, there are buildings out there that have lots of cans of food in them? And you can go trade for them?"

"*Take* 'em man! You can go take 'em!" Fitzgerald picked up the can and waved it at me. "They don't *belong* to anybody anymore. You just walk in and take 'em!"

Fitzgerald watched me to see if I understood. "You have to realize," he said, "that at one time there were millions of human beings living in this city—millions! That means there's a lot of food left in the stores for us porcupines. And there's plenty in the Skunk District, too. It's not just food, either. There are clothes, toys, tools, weapons. . . ."

He stopped. "Well," he said. "It's hard to find knives anymore. And jewelry. The Dragon Lady sent her ratminks to collect all the jewels in the city. Pretty useless, if you ask me. For some reason she's crazy about jewels. She doesn't care a bit about the canned food. True predators don't, you know.

"This place used to be a store," he said. "A bookstore. My grandfather took it over because he thought somebody should make sure the books didn't get eaten or burned for fuel.

"It's my place now," he added. "I've got a pretty complete record of human life here."

So *that's* what was in the books. A record of human life!

"Are all the books true?" I asked Fitzgerald.

"Oh, no," he said. "A lot of them are fantasy. But then, some fantasies have more truth to them than factual books do."

"What do you mean?" I asked.

"Well, here's an example. According to most of the so-called factual books, animals couldn't talk. But then, in a good fantasy, like *The Wind in the Willows* for instance, the animals are all talking— the same as you and me! So you tell me, which is more true?"

I couldn't answer that.

Instead I said, "Back home I tell stories at the All-Forest Meets—old legends about humans and ancient times, and far-off places. My sister, Dolores, says they aren't true, but you know what? There's one about the City of Ruins, and here it is—a real place!

"Well, there you go," said Fitzgerald.

I licked the peach juice off my paw and wiped down my front.

"Do you think I'll be able to get home from here?" I asked him.

"Sure," he said. "We'll figure something out."

He stroked the whiskers on his chin. "It'll be a long trip, you know," he finally said. "And upriver this time. Let me think about it. Right now what you need is some sleep."

That's when I noticed how tired I was.

Fitzgerald made up a bed for me on the table. I dragged my aching body over the side and nuzzled under the cloth. "Thanks," I mumbled.

There was a little click, and the room went dark.

I jumped up. "WAIT!" I shouted.

There was another click, and it got light again. "What's the matter? Are you afraid of the dark?"

"Huh? Oh, no. Of course not! But just tell me one thing, is that an electric light?"

Fitzgerald stared at me. He smiled and covered his mouth with his paw.

"Yes," he said after a moment, "it's an electric light. I've got solar panels on the roof."

He turned the light off again, and I was asleep before he had left the room.

After my bath the next morning we ate *canned nuts.*

Then Fitzgerald gave me a book to read. It was about Dick and Jane, the human children. It even had pictures.

I stared at the pictures. It was *all true.* The humans always wore clothes, and they didn't have any fur on their bodies, just on their heads. But not on their whole heads. I didn't know the faces would be bare too.

I learned a lot from that book.

The words in the Dick and Jane book were easy. With a little help I could read it myself.

Fitzgerald said I was pretty smart for a small animal. He said if I practiced,

I'd be able to read anything!

When Fitzgerald was busy, I looked at the books on the shelves. I sounded out some of the titles, and I wondered what they were all about. *The Mill on the Floss.* (What's floss?) *A Little Princess.* (Dolores would like that.) *Wild Animals I Have Known.* . . .

I wondered, *What if I stayed here forever? . . . And read all these books . . . and ate food out of cans!*

I poked around behind the shelves and nosed out a cozy spot for a future sleeping chamber. There was even some old paper I might be able to use for bedding.

Then I started thinking about Mom and Dolores.

I bet they were worried about me. They probably thought I had drowned.

"Thelonious!" Fitzgerald called me.

"I'm coming!" I crawled out from my cozy spot.

"Let's go see some friends," he said. "And I'll show you around."

"Oh," I said. "I'd love to, except . . . well . . . the thing is, I noticed how everybody around here wears clothes, and I haven't got any!"

Fitzgerald laughed. "No problem," he said. "We can stop and get you some."

Cool. Just like that!

5

On the Road

53

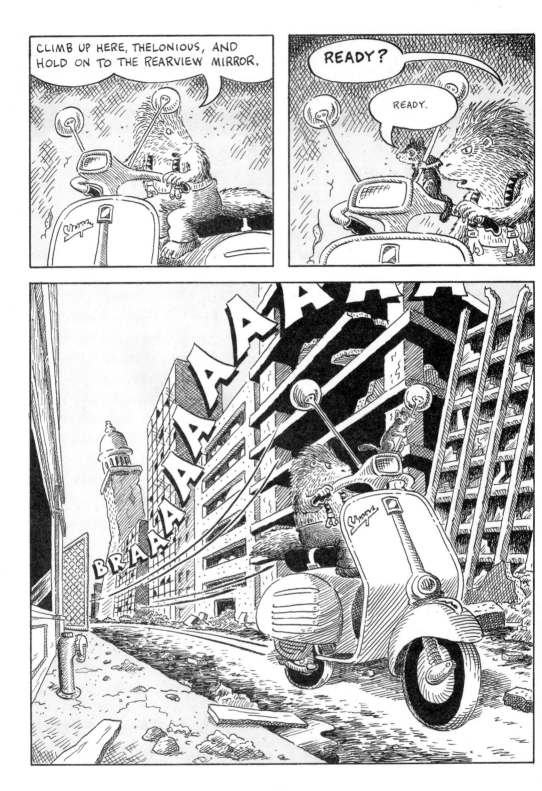

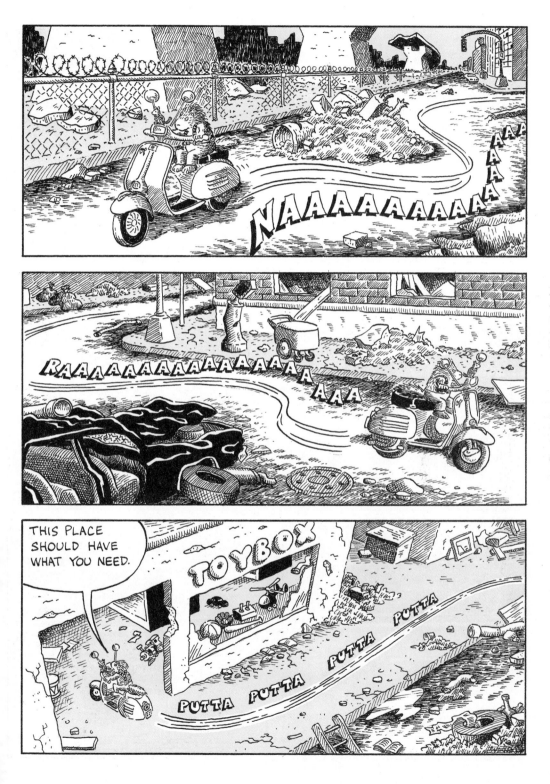

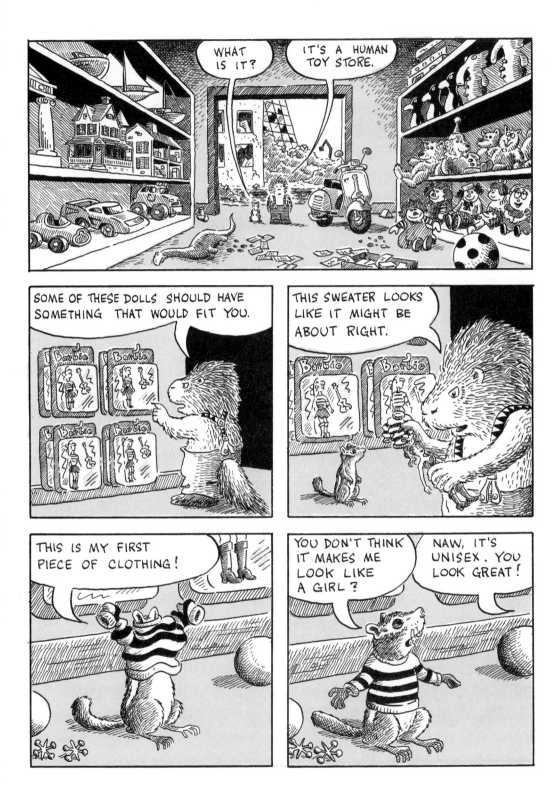

6

Wally's Story

"The FLYING Bear?" Fitzgerald said. And I laughed.

"That's funny," I said. "You're kidding, right?"

But Wally bristled his quills and said, "Hey, would I kid you? No, it's true all right. Ask anybody. The bear flew here—in a flying machine."

Fitzgerald shook his head, "A *flying machine*? No way!"

"Why not?" Wally said. "The *humans* had flying machines, Fitz. Airplanes. You've got a book on them up at your place—*Airplanes of the World*, or something. I've seen it."

"Yeah, but that's humans," Fitzgerald said.

"All right," Wally shrugged his rough shoulders. "Don't believe me." He folded his arms and clamped his mouth shut.

But I wanted to hear about the flying bear. I said, "I believe you, Wally."

Wally smiled at me. "I saw her with my own eyes, Thelonious. I heard the roar of an engine, and a shadow passed over me, so I looked up. . . .

"There was a *machine* up there, putt-putting across the sky! I was staring at it. I remembered that book I had seen at your place, Fitz, and I was wondering if I could really be looking at an airplane, when the engine noise stopped dead."

He made a chopping motion with his paw. "Silence," he said. "The machine just hung there for a second, and then it started corkscrewing down. And *then*, with a big *BWOOM!* it exploded!

"I thought it was the end of the world, at first. There was fire in the sky, and sparks shooting out. I really thought it was all over .

And *then*, as if all that wasn't strange enough, this *bear* comes floating down with a parachute, splashes into the river, swims ashore, shakes herself off, and walks away.

"I tell you, it took me a week to recover," he finished.

Fitzgerald frowned at Wally. "Why didn't I hear about this?" he asked.

"Who knows?" Wally shrugged. "Sometimes we don't see you down here for weeks. You probably had your snout in a book.

"Anyway, getting back to the bear, I wasn't the only one who saw her come down, you know. Some of the others that saw her started a rumor that she's a witch, but I don't know about that.

"I've seen her around since then. She's got a workshop set up in an old warehouse down on Jay Street. The word is that she's building a new flying machine."

Fitzgerald gave Wally a piercing look. "I don't know, Wally," he said. "Maybe, just *maybe*, she found an old flying machine and figured out how to fly it. Although I wouldn't believe that if you hadn't seen it yourself. But now she's supposed to be *building* one? I don't think so."

"I'm not saying it's true," Wally said. "I'm telling you what I've heard, that's all."

Fitzgerald thought about it. "You'd have to have the tools. And the knowledge. And thumbs. You'd have to have thumbs to use the tools. And bears don't have thumbs. Only porcupines and skunks have thumbs."

I said, "I have thumbs." I held one up. Two pairs of beady, porcupine eyes looked at my thumb. "That surprises me," Fitzgerald finally said. "Are thumbs common in the Untamed Forest?"

"No," I said. "Some of the animals make fun of them, but I don't mind because they come in handy. My friend Victor, he says it means I was descended from a lab animal."

"A lab animal!" snorted Fitzgerald. "I never heard of chipmunks being used for lab animals. Or porcupines, either! No, it's evolution. Thumbs just make good evolutionary sense. It's a wonder all animals don't have them!"

"Like bears?" I said.

Wally laughed. "Fitz thinks he knows everything because he's read so many books," he said to me. "But there's a lot to be learned outside of books too."

"Okay," grunted Fitzgerald. "So we'll admit this bear might have thumbs, and she *might* be building a flying machine. What else do you know about her, Wally?"

"She comes from a place called the Fog Mound. At least that's how she introduces herself—Olive Bear of the Fog Mound. Of course, most of us think of her as the Flying Bear, or the Witch Bear."

"I think of her as the Bear of the Mist," I said.

"Nice name," said Wally.

"So, where is this Fog Mound?" grunted Fitzgerald. "I never heard of it."

"As I understand it, even the bear isn't sure where it is. Her flying machine got blown off course by a storm. She lost her sense of direction and didn't know where she was when she came down."

Just like me, I thought.

Fitzgerald must have been thinking the same thing. "It's funny, isn't it," he said. "Two unusual animals, a chipmunk and a bear, both turn up here, driven by storms."

"Pretty risky business, this flying," said Wally.

"I'll say," agreed Fitzgerald. "Unless you're a bird."

He scratched his head. "I'm wondering about the Fog Mound, though. What kind of a place would have old human flying machines lying around? Did you ever hear of any place like that, Wally?"

"You're the expert," Wally said to him. "Personally, I don't claim to know what else is out there. It's a big world. There could be any number of strange things going on that we don't know about.

"Look at Thelonious here, with his thumbs," he added. "Who would have guessed that a talking chipmunk with thumbs lived in the Untamed Forest!"

"I've heard of the Fog Mound too," I said proudly.

"You have?" Fitzgerald sounded surprised. "Oh, it must have been in one of those legends you were telling me about."

"No, it's from your place, Fitzgerald. There's an old book down behind the bookcase. At first I thought it was just bedding material, but then I saw it had letters on the front. 'A Way of Life,' it said, by somebody Bear of The Fog Mound."

"He *reads*, too?" Wally said to Fitzgerald.

To me he said, "What did you find out about the Fog Mound, Thelonious?"

"Nothing," I apologized. "I'm not a very good reader. I need more practice. But anyway, when I looked inside the book, there weren't any more letters. Just a lot of squiggly lines."

"Sounds like cursive," Wally said. "Does he know cursive?" he asked Fitzgerald.

Fitzgerald made some marks in the dirt. "Did it look like this?" he asked me.

I looked at the marks. "Well, sort of. I wasn't paying too much attention, you know."

I tried to describe what the book was like. "It wasn't like a real book," I said. "More just a bunch of pages inside a soft cover. And the pages had holes on one side. And there were rings that went through the holes and held everything together."

"A notebook, written in cursive. Hmmm." Fitzgerald tapped a claw against one of his teeth. "Maybe it came in with that pile of papers Huber found in the cellar of his new place. I never got a chance to look through them."

"Wasn't that over a year ago, now?" asked Wally.

Fitzgerald ignored that. "You know what?' he continued. "This whole bear story is pretty interesting. I think I'd like to meet Olive Bear of the Fog Mound. Down on Jay Street, is that what you said, Wally?"

"Two blocks over and three blocks down," Wally said, nodding. "Just past the old parking garage."

Fitzgerald drained his bowl and put it down. "Thanks for the broth, Wally." To me he said, "How'd you like to go meet your Bear of the Mist, Thelonious."

"Uh, not very much," I said. "Bears and chipmunks, we don't mix much."

Fitzgerald just laughed. "Don't worry. You'll be safe with me. Nobody messes with porcupines."

7

TAP
TAP

The Bear of the Mist

73

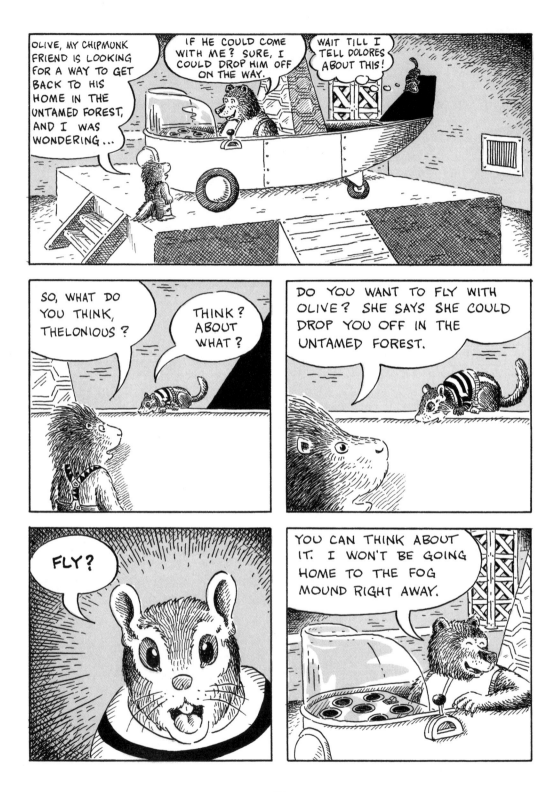

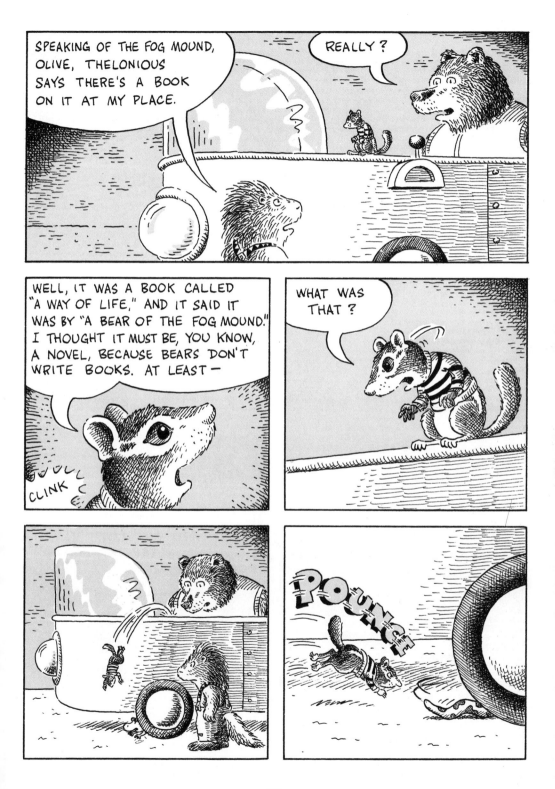

76

Dear Diary...

The book was still there. I dragged it out, and handed it to Fitzgerald. He put it on the table. It was called,

A WAY OF LIFE By Ragna Bear of the Fog Mound

"RAGNA!" roared Olive, pointing to the name with one of her huge claws.

I jumped backward.

I had never been so close to a bear's paw. The fur on it was long and thick and lay flat like marsh grass. The claw was like a sword.

"Sorry," she apologized more quietly. "I was just surprised, because Ragna is my *sister!* I never guessed there would be something written by her.

"I've got two sisters," she explained. "Ragna and Ruby. Ruby is the oldest, and she was the first to be told the Secret Way. Did I tell you about the Secret Way?"

Fitzgerald and I shook our heads.

"You haven't told us anything," I said.

"Oh," grunted Olive. "Okay, let me explain."

She picked up Ragna's book and sank heavily into one of Fitzgerald's chairs.

I noticed that the chair, which seemed *humongous* to me, was just the right

 size for Olive. In fact, she fitted in it much better than Fitzgerald did, and it was his chair. Or was it?

And then I had a revelation! It was a *human's* chair, like everything else around here. And that meant that the *human beings* must have been big too—as big as bears! Not (as I had always thought) small like me. *Duh!*

Well, that explained a whole lot.

"Okay," said Olive, "so you know that the Mound is surrounded by a belt of deadly fog, right?"

No, we didn't know that, either.

"Well, it is. That's why it's called the Fog Mound.

"The Mound itself is a hill, or a plateau really, in the middle of a mountain range. It's completely surrounded by deadly fog, so nobody can get in or out— not unless they know the Secret Way. That keeps the Mound safe from intruders, you see."

"They get lost in the fog?" I piped up.

"Worse than that. The fog makes them crazy and draws them in, deeper and deeper, until they fall asleep and never wake up. 'Once in, never out,'" quoted Olive in a low, solemn tone, "that's what they say about the fog.

"However," she continued, "there is a *Secret Way*, known only to the grown-up bears. When they think you're old enough, your parents reveal it to you. Then you can go into the outside world and roam."

Olive showed her big teeth in a startling grin. "Young bears like to roam a bit," she explained.

"Some Fog Mound bears find mates during their roaming and come back to live on the Fog Mound and raise their families. And some come back alone and are just aunts and uncles. That's how it's been for generations and generations.

"So Ruby, my oldest sister, got told the Secret Way, and she went away.

"And the next year Ragna, my second sister, got told the Secret Way, and *she* went away.

"And I stayed at home, waiting for it to be my turn.

"But Ruby didn't come back, and Ragna didn't come back either. And when it was time for me to go, my parents said I had to wait until one of the others returned—they wouldn't tell me the Secret Way! I ask you, is that fair?"

She glared at us and said, "No! It is not. So, after a while I just got tired of waiting, and I built a flying machine!"

"You *built* it?" said Fitzgerald. "But, how?"

"Well, the Cliff House library has a lot of books. There wasn't one specifically on how to build an airplane, but there *was* one on how things fly and another one on the history of manned flight. I got the idea of flying from those books.

"And then I found an old model plane kit, still in its box, in the toy cupboard. I guess nobody before me had the patience to build it. But I did, and I learned a lot from it. So after reading the books and practicing on the model, I enlarged the plans, and I was able to build a simple airplane. I'm good with engines, so that was no problem. I just took one out of an old mower."

I felt confused. Model plane kit? Enlarged the plans? Good with engines? What did it all mean?

Olive continued, "I didn't know whether the thing would get off the ground or not. But after a few tries it did! I took it right up over the trees and over the fog, and then I just kept on going.

"I had never flown before, and I had never been off the Mound before, so you can imagine how excited I was. I didn't notice the storm clouds gathering until I was in the middle of them. Then I lost my sense of direction. I came out of the storm flying over this strange city, the plane exploded, and here I am. But where *here* is, in relation to *there* . . ." She shrugged her massive shoulders. "I haven't got a clue."

Fitzgerald and I remained silent.

I didn't know what *he* was thinking, but *I* was still stuck on what it meant to be "good with engines."

"Well." Olive straightened in her chair. "Now that you have a little background, let's see what Ragna has to say."

She opened the book. "Oh, look." She laughed. "It starts, 'Dear Diary'! Isn't it just like Ragna to keep a diary!"

After a few minutes I said, "What else does it say?"

"Oh, sorry," said Olive. "I'll read it out loud."

Dear Diary, she read. *Sometimes I think about Debartelo Bear. I'm sure he liked me. I think he would have asked me to marry him if I had encouraged him. How different my life would have been! We would be back home by now. Back on the Fog Mound with Mother and Pubba.*

"Pubba is our father," she stopped to explained.

Instead, I had to go looking for somebody better—more handsome, more exciting, more fun. And Debartelo was such a sweet bear. Well, look at me now! Dying of a putrid fever in this dreary hovel in the City of Ruins, with a dragon lizard's bite on my foot and only my memories to keep me warm. Oh, woe is me!

Fitzgerald exclaimed, "A dragon lizard's bite! That can be deadly!"

"Oh, I doubt if it was that bad," Olive said. "Ragna would have had her medicine bag. And she always has to dramatize everything. Who else do you know says, 'Oh, woe is me'?"

She continued reading:

Never again do I expect to see my beloved Fog Mound, where I spent the happy days of my youth in the loving company of my family and friends, where we all had learned to read and write, to grow and preserve our own food, and to live well off the bounty of the land.

In these pages I hope to describe the wonderful way of life that I have forsaken and, in so doing, relive the lost joys of my childhood!

Olive turned the page and stopped. She flipped through the following pages.

"Don't stop there!" I said. "What happens next?"

"There isn't any next," Olive said. "The rest of the pages are blank."

"Blank? Let's see." Fitzgerald flipped through the book himself. "You're right," he said. "I wonder if that means . . . well . . . a dragon lizard's bite. . . ." He touched Olive gently on the back of her paw. "I'm sorry," he said.

"It looks bad, doesn't it?" Olive said in a small voice. "I guess she wouldn't have just abandoned her diary, unless she had to."

I knew what they were thinking. Ragna must have died before she could write any more.

There was a moment of silence, while we each thought our own thoughts about death, and lost sisters, and dragon lizard bites.

"Ahem." Fitzgerald changed the subject. "Grow your own food there, do you?" he said. "I don't know of any other agricultural communities of animals. What's it really like?"

Olive rested her paws on her belly and looked thoughtful.

"The sky is big," she said at last. "From the roof of Cliff House you can watch the sun set over rows of distant mountains. On summer evenings fireflies twinkle at the edge of the woods, where the trees are tall and produce many nuts. The water is cool and fresh and pure—good for swimming in and delicious for drinking. The fields are broad and hum with bees in the sun."

I thought, *Except for the part about the Cliff House roof, she might be describing the Untamed Forest!* And I wished I was home.

After a few moments Olive pulled her lips back from her teeth again, in that scary grin, and said, "If *I* was writing a diary about the Fog Mound, I would tell about the candy room in Cliff House, where Mother makes caramels. It's got a big table with a marble top. She pours thick steaming caramel syrup onto the marble, where it oozes slowly up to some heavy metal bars and smoothes out, all flat and creamy and golden tan. Then, when it's almost cool, Mother takes away the metal bars, and with the long two-handled knife she cuts it into squares—*fwop, fwop* this way and *fwop, fwop* that way. And if we help wrap the squares in waxed paper, we each get one to taste—still slightly warm and soft in the center, and buttery sweet. Mmmmm."

She closed her eyes and rested her head on the back of the chair.

"And I would tell about the library, full of books," she continued. "And the big couch in the window alcove that sags to the floor from all the bears who have lain on it, reading and dreaming their winter afternoons away. And I would tell about playing charades by the fire on a snowy evening, laughing so hard it hurts, while Ruby tries to act out a hard word, like 'forensic.'"

Olive laughed at the memory.

Fitzgerald smiled too. He said, "The diary says all the animals learn to read and write, but what about the non-talkers?"

"Oh, there aren't any non-talkers on the Fog Mound," said Olive. "Well, except for the insects and worms and mussels and fish and so on."

Fitzgerald stared at her for a few moments, taking it in.

"Tell me about the growing-your-own-food part of the Fog Mound," he said.

"Ah, yes," said Olive. "Our lives are centered around the growing and preserving of food, and there's always plenty. More than enough. Everyone helps, and that's what makes it work. The cows donate milk. The birds raise a few chicks, but then they produce unfertilized eggs for cooking. The small animals collect seeds and start seedlings and do bug control. The midsized animals help make preserves and run the storage cellars. The large animals drive the tractors and do the harvesting. We often all get together to eat at Cliff House, and my mom is a great cook!"

I sighed. It sounded pretty nice there.

"Of course, we're all vegetarians on the Fog Mound," Olive added.

"All vegetarians!" I squeaked. "You mean there are no *predators?*"

"That's right," she said. "Well, insects and grubs are considered fair game, and freshwater mussels. You know, all those things I mentioned before."

I nodded. I liked the occasional grub myself. But still! "No cats?" I asked, just to make sure. "Or dogs or wolves or foxes?"

"Oh, we've got some small cats and dogs, and some foxes, too. They eat milk and cheese and eggs and vegetables, just like we bears do. There's plenty to eat and no need to kill your fellow animals."

A short, awed silence was broken by the slam of the back door.

Fitzgerald jumped up, saying, "Drat! I must have forgotten to lock the door!"

We all rushed out to look, but there was nobody there.

Fitzgerald took a peek in his cupboard. "I don't see anything missing," he said.

"What's that?" I said, pointing at a piece of paper on the dining table. "That wasn't there this morning."

Fitzgerald picked it up. "It looks like a letter," he said, unfolding the piece of paper. He studied it, then read it out loud.

"That brown lizard!" I snarled. "It's probably a trap!"

DRAGON LADY AND RATMINKS PLAN TO ATTACK WAREHOUSE TOMORROW NIGHT AND STEAL FLYING MACHINE. BURN THIS NOTE.   BROWN LIZARD

"Why do you say that?" asked Fitzgerald.

"I don't trust that spying lizard," I said. "Why does he keep following us around? And why would he want to warn us of an attack? I'll bet it's not even true."

90

Fitzgerald reread the note. "Maybe not," he said. "But then again, if it *is* true, and we don't take some kind of action, Olive will certainly lose her flying machine, if not worse! Remember what a dragon lizard did to Ragna. No, I think we should take this note seriously. But that said,"—he paused,—"I'm not sure what we can do. We certainly aren't prepared to fight thousands of ratminks!"

Thousands?

"Hmmm, didn't he say it's tomorrow night?" said Olive. "I wonder if I can be ready to leave before then. Let's see, I've got to get the solar panels from the roof and install them. And pack up anything I want to take. Oh, and make some kind of harness for Thelonious. You do want to get dropped off in the Untamed Forest, don't you, Thelonious?"

Fitzgerald was busy burning the lizard's note. When I didn't answer right away, he turned and said, "It's a great opportunity, Thelonious. A quick ride home, and the chance to fly! Oh, boy, I almost wish I was going too!"

He stared off into space.

"Watch out!" Olive cried.

"Oops!" Fitzgerald dropped the flaming paper. The fire quickly died out, leaving a little pile of ashes and the smell of burning fur.

"No biggy," said Fitzgerald, rubbing his paw on his pants.

Olive and Fitzgerald both turned to me, waiting for my answer.

Rats, I thought. *I want to go home, sure. But chipmunks don't fly. Bears don't fly either. And neither do big machines made out of metal, like that one in Olive's warehouse.* Birds *fly.*

Besides, I'm not sure I want to go home yet. Fitzgerald is pretty cool. He was going to help me practice my reading, and I was planning on going to some more stores and maybe getting some more clothes and stuff.

Olive was all ready to go. She was waiting at the door, holding Ragna's diary and looking at me, and I had to decide.

I decided I would say no. I opened my mouth to speak, but Olive spoke first.

"I'll admit there is some risk, Thelonious," she said. "But not as much as on my last trip. Now that I've had some experience with flying, I don't anticipate any problems at all. The last machine was one I made from scratch, you know, out of wood and cloth. But my new machine is metal, and it's made from a human kit. As long as there's a meadow or some flat, open area in the Untamed Forest where I can land, we should be fine."

Oh good, I thought. *She's going to land.* I had been worried about getting "dropped off."

Olive looked at me with kind eyes, waiting.

"There is a meadow," I said slowly, seeing the old, familiar field in my mind.

I jumped off the table, suddenly excited about going home, about seeing Mom and Dolores and everyone. *Wait till I tell them about all this!*

"Okay," I said. "I'll do it!"

Olive held out her paw to Fitzgerald. "I'm sorry to leave so soon after meeting you, Fitzgerald," she began.

Instead of touching her paw, Fitzgerald turned away and looked out the window.

"You know," he said slowly, "I've been thinking too. I'm not that young, and I've never traveled much. I thought . . . well . . . that is, I was wondering if you would mind, Olive, if I went along as well. All the way to the Fog Mound, I mean."

Olive started to say something, but Fitzgerald held up his hand to stop her.

"I know we might not make it," he said. "I know there's a chance you won't be able to find the place, even. Or there could be a problem with the machine, or the weather. *Anything* could happen. I know that. But the thing is, I see this as my big chance! My chance for adventure, to see the world, to experience life outside the City of Ruins! To *fly*! And to see the Fog Mound itself. How can I pass up a chance for all that? If you'll have me, that is."

Olive smiled. "I'd be happy to have your company," she said.

I smiled too. I was glad Fitzgerald was going.

He had some things to do to get ready, so Olive went back to the warehouse alone, and we followed later.

As we drove through the rubble, I looked around at the huge buildings and I thought, *This is really me, Thelonious Chipmunk, riding on a motor scooter with a talking porcupine. I'm in the City of Ruins. All of this stuff was built by humans.*

And I'm wearing a sweater that I got in a toy store! I would never forget this.

Back at the warehouse we prepared for our trip.

There was one night and one day before we were supposed to get attacked (at least according to that lizard, who probably had some cunning plan of his own).

Olive was working on the velocicopter, adding a special seat for me.

If you asked me, I didn't think it would ever get off the ground. But Olive and Fitzgerald seemed to believe in it, so I didn't say anything.

Fitzgerald and I helped load supplies.

Looking around her warehouse, Olive said, "I hate leaving so much good stuff behind, but easy come, easy go, I guess. Maybe the ratminks can use it.

Thelonious, do you want any small souvenirs to take back to the Untamed Forest?"

Do I?

I found a nice piece of soft cloth for my mother and a small, shiny chain for Dolores. And to show them what the humans had looked like, I tore a picture out of a book.

"What about for yourself?" said Olive. "Isn't there something you've always wanted?"

I thought about it.

"There's a legend I like," I said. "It's about a rock of rainbow colors. I always thought that would be a cool thing to have. You haven't got a rock of rainbow colors, have you?"

"A rock of rainbow colors," Olive repeated thoughtfully.

Fitzgerald said, "Most of the rocks around here are pretty gray. I know! How about a marble? Have you got any marbles, Olive?"

Olive smiled. "Not here," she said.

"Never mind," I said. "It was just an idea. Could I take the picture off of a can

of peaches, instead? It would be a good replacement for my postcard."

Fitzgerald helped me soak a can so the picture would come off. We dried it, then rolled it up with Dolores's picture and chain, and wrapped everything in Mom's cloth.

Olive worked late that night and most of the following day, checking her instruments, tightening bolts, and going through her manual.

Fitzgerald went over to Wally's place. He wanted to say good-bye and to leave Wally the scooter and the keys to the bookshop. When he got back, he helped Olive with the solar panels.

I didn't have anything to do, so I tried to practice my reading in a book Olive had. It was called *Fundamental Aeronautics*. I didn't get very far.

Then I looked at Ragna's diary.

I wished I knew cursive.

I turned over the blank pages to see if we had missed anything. I noticed there was a kind of a flap inside the front cover, so I pried it open and stuck my head in.

9

Attack of the Ratminks

100

101

107

10

Night Flight

I held on tight to my harness, feeling sick. I felt the velocicopter tilt and turn. Ooooooh.

"Hey, what are you doing?" Fitzgerald shouted to Olive.

I opened my eyes. There was nothing but air between me and the City of Ruins far below.

I closed my eyes again.

"I'm going back!" Olive replied. "We've got to get those maps."

"But we don't need them anymore, do we?" shouted Fitzgerald. "You know the way now. And we won't need the other map—the one to the Secret Way—because we'll be flying *over* the fog. Isn't that right?"

"*We* might not need those maps," Olive said. "But I don't want anyone else finding them either. They reveal too much!"

We headed back toward Olive's old warehouse—where a column of smoke was now rising out of the roof—back toward the Dragon Lady and the horrible ratminks.

"I don't know, Olive," Fitzgerald was saying, "I think maybe we should forget about the maps. It's too smoky to land on the roof, and . . ."

FWOOM. A huge fireball shot up through the warehouse roof, and a lot of animals ran out of the burning building. From where I sat, they looked like tiny ants. "Haha! Take that, you ant-sized ratminks!" I shouted.

"YOW!" cried Olive. "That must have been my fuel cans exploding! Fitzgerald, what if it burns down the whole city?"

"I don't think you need to worry about that," Fitzgerald replied. "There's nothing but a lot of stone and concrete around there. The fire will soon burn itself out."

Olive took the machine higher and circled once over the fire.

"Anyway," she said, "I guess those maps are toast now."

So, we headed north again, leaving the fire and smoke behind.

In the west the red sun sank over the hills, and then the light of day faded from the sky.

It was cold. I pulled the sleeves of my sweater down over my paws.

The moon came up, and the sky was spattered with stars. In the distance you could see where the dark glow of the sky met the solid black of the land. All around us the soft clouds reflected the moonlight.

It was beautiful, and the machine was going like a dream.

I could hardly believe it—*me*, up in the sky, *flying*!

We followed the river north. Already we were far beyond the City of Ruins. Somewhere ahead of us lay the Untamed Forest. And Mom. And Dolores.

A rough hand clamped over my mouth. And a voice in my ear whispered, "Don't yell. It's only me."

Mmmf! I couldn't yell even if I'd wanted to. So I bit.

There was a smothered yelp, the hand was jerked away, and I whipped my head around to see who it was.

It was that spying lizard! A renewed attack!

"Don't worry," the lizard whispered. "I'm alone."

"What are you doing here?" I whispered back.

"Going to the Fog Mound, what else?"

"Oh, yeah?" I said out loud. "Well, I don't remember anybody inviting you!"

"Shhh."

"They can't hear us," I said. "We're downwind."

The lizard sat beside me, hanging onto the bars of my platform.

"You're supposed to be strapped in," I muttered. "What if we hit some air turbulence?"

"Right. Well, I suppose I could squeeze in with you," he said. And he did, before I could even stop him.

"After you saw me in the warehouse," he hissed into my ear, "I slipped out and hid on the porcupine's scooter. Then I followed you into the book-shop."

I squirmed, trying to put some distance between me and the obnoxious lizard.

"I heard you guys talking about it," he continued. "The Fog Mound, I mean. I got the idea right away. Why do you think I gave you that note?"

His round reptilian eyes peered into mine, but he answered his own question. "I realized it was my big chance to escape from the Dragon Lady, that's why! And I knew that if she could get a hold of the flying machine, like she was planning to do, I would have lost my chance!"

"But you're her spy," I said.

"Not anymore," he said. "Didn't you hear me? I escaped!"

He stuck out his hand. "Call me Brown," he said.

I glared at him. But I shook his hand.

"All right," I said. "If that's what you want."

"I don't know about want," he said. "It's my name."

"Oh. Well, how do you do, Brown," I said.

"What do you mean, how do I do?" he asked.

"It doesn't mean anything. It's what you say when you meet someone, that's all," I explained.

"We met a long time ago. And I don't know why you say something that doesn't mean anything."

"But we didn't exchange names before," I said.

"I know your name. It's Thelonious. I've known it for a long time."

"Yeah, but . . . Oh, forget it."

I frowned at him. "I don't know what Olive will say about you hitching a ride," I muttered.

"I thought *you* could tell her," said Brown. "That's why I came up here first.

"It's cold, isn't it?" he added. "I'm an ectotherm, you know. That means I need to get my heat from my environment. I get kind of sluggish in the cold. But you give off a lot of heat, so I guess I'll be okay."

His head slumped down on my shoulder, and he started sleeping.

He's got a lot of nerve! I thought.

The velocicopter leaned and turned. I looked down. I was surprised to see that we were already over the Untamed Forest.

I could see the tops of the trees in the moonlight. I could see the Big Oak and Sunny Meadow. In fact, I knew right where we were!

Olive was circling. She had spotted the meadow too, and she was going down!

Olive set the velocicopter down gently into the tall moonlit grass and turned off the engine.

Suddenly it was totally quiet.

I was home.

11

Home

125

THAT NIGHT, WHILE OLIVE AND FITZGERALD AND BROWN LIZARD SLEPT OUT UNDER THE STARS, I TOLD MY MOTHER AND DOLORES ALL ABOUT MY ADVENTURES IN THE CITY OF RUINS.

I ALWAYS KNEW YOU WERE SPECIAL, THELONIOUS!

OH, POOH! HE'S LUCKY TO BE ALIVE AND BACK HOME WHERE HE BELONGS!

I'M NOT SURE THIS **IS** WHERE I BELONG, DOLORES.

IN FACT...

12

The Crash

Here's something I learned from flying: The sky is bigger than the land!

At first I couldn't take my eyes off the view—the glittering river, the rounded treetops, the distant hills. But then I got sleepy.

When I woke up, we were *still* flying.

There wasn't much to do up there. It was cold, I was hungry, and Brown was crowding me. The view was pretty much the same.

I slept some more.

I woke up feeling stiff and seriously hungry.

"Move over," I grumbled to the sleeping lizard, giving him a shove. It didn't bother him a bit. He slumped right back against me.

Olive and Fitzgerald were talking. Fitzgerald pointed to the right. Olive nodded and adjusted our direction. I looked to see what they were talking about, but all I could see ahead of us was another misty mountaintop.

Then I sat up, straight and alert. *A misty mountaintop!* Wasn't that what we were looking for?

We were heading straight for it. Fitzgerald turned back to look at me. He pointed and shouted, "That's it! The Fog Mound! We made it!"

At the first jolt I was completely taken by surprise.

Confused, I watched a large rock bounce off us and roll across the sky.

When the second rock hit, we tilted sideways, then plunged headfirst

toward the ground. I screamed. Brown woke up and grabbed me around the neck in a stranglehold. I could hardly breathe.

"Leggo!" I squeaked, pounding him off with my fists.

There was another, gentler, jolt. The machine righted itself, and we hung there, suspended under a large silver canopy. It was the emergency rapid-descent reduction system! We were saved!

Slowly we drifted down, saved by our silver parachute.

Nobody spoke.

Even after we had settled into the branches of a tall tree and the rapid-descent reduction system had crumpled down behind us, nobody spoke.

Then Olive said, "Is everyone all right? . . . Fitzgerald?"

Fitzgerald grunted, "Yup."

"Thelonious? Brown?"

"We're okay," I said. "What happened?"

Olive looked up and pointed to two dark silhouettes that were flying off into the distance.

"Birds?" asked Fitzgerald.

"Eagles," said Olive. "It looks like they dropped some big rocks on us."

She hung her head. "I'm sorry. I was so excited to get home, I forgot all about them. Last spring, when I *left* the Mound, I was careful to fly the other way because I knew they wouldn't like a flying machine approaching their nest. But I didn't even think of it today.

"Look, you can see the nest from here."

I looked and saw the eagles' tree—bare branches sticking up out of the

fog, with a big tangle of a nest at the top. It gave me the shivers.

"They don't hunt on the Mound," Olive said, as if she sensed my fear. "Their ancestors signed a pact with my ancestors. And of course, they wouldn't have expected it to be me who was flying in the velocicopter."

"We must have seemed like a huge flying monster coming after their nest."

Fitzgerald looked up at the bent rotor blades. "I wonder how much damage they did."

Olive grasped the back of her seat and turned her huge bulk around to look. The whole flying machine lurched sideways.

I grabbed my harness.

Branches cracked, then snapped, and we crashed through another ten feet or so of tree before coming to rest again on some stronger branches.

"Oops," gasped Olive. "Sorry, guys. I guess you three had better clear out before I try that again. Thelonious, can you and Brown get out?"

I started undoing the harness. "Brown's asleep," I said.

I gave him a little shove. "Wake up, Brown."

He opened his eyes, looked around, closed them again, and said, "Cold . . . sleep."

"He's an ectotherm," I explained.

"That's okay," Fitzgerald said. "You go ahead, Thelonious. I can carry Brown."

I got out of the harness, leaving Brown behind, and climbed along a branch to where it met the tree's big trunk. I huddled there, against the trunk, trying not to look down. I'm not really a tall-tree animal—not like a gray squirrel, for instance. And speaking of gray squirrels, I hadn't seen or heard another soul. We must have scared them all away.

I watched Fitzgerald climb carefully out of his seat. He pawed through some boxes and collected a few supplies, while Olive sat still. Then he lifted the limp Brown into his pack and joined me at the trunk. The machine had not shifted again.

"You three go all the way down," called Olive. "And stand well away from the tree, while I get the velocicopter down. I'm going to cut free the chute and shake the branches."

"What are you, nuts!" cried Fitzgerald. "You'll kill yourself! Just leave it."

"I'll be careful," Olive assured him. "We need the velocicopter to get to the Mound, and there's no way I can fix it up here. I'll get it down somehow, and then I'll see what we can salvage. Just give me a whistle when you're safely away. Go on!"

"All right," Fitzgerald muttered. "Stubborn bear."

I followed him down as closely as I could, holding on to the rough bark and slithering from branch to branch. I felt better when we finally reached solid ground and hurried to a safe spot beneath another tree.

Fitzgerald let out an unearthly, loud, high-pitched whistle.

I yelped and covered my ears, but it was too late. "You should have warned me," I said.

Olive heard him. The whole world probably heard him.

Then there came a lot of noise from up high in the tree—horrible cracking sounds and noises of things falling through branches.

Brown slept on.

"LOOK OUT BELOW!" Olive finally bellowed.

Fitz and I backed up against our tree. Moments later the flying machine hit the ground with a sickening *THUNK!* It was followed by a shower of twigs and leaves.

Olive followed at a slower pace. I could see the branches swaying as she squeezed her way down.

Fitz and I went over to see what was left of the velocicopter.

He shook his head. "No way she's fixing that machine," he said. "Not without tools, anyway."

Olive jumped down the last few feet and joined us.

I thought we made a pretty sorry looking group, standing there in the wilderness beside our pile of twisted metal.

Olive didn't say anything more about fixing the flying machine. She didn't say anything at all.

A cold wind blew through the trees.

I shivered and was glad I wasn't alone.

"What do we do now?" I said.

Olive turned away. "I think I'll take a nap," she muttered. "This cold weather is making me sleepy."

"Yeah, me too," I said, yawning and checking out our surroundings. "Let's find a nice hole. . . ." I looked at Olive's bulk. "Or a cave," I amended. "We can make plans tomorrow."

"Oh, no you don't," said Fitzgerald. "I know what will happen if I let you two go to sleep. You won't wake up until spring, just like Brown here! No, we'll make a fire. There's plenty of dry wood around. Olive, you get some of those bigger branches. Thelonious and I will get the kindling. Hup, hup!"

"Bossy, isn't he?" Olive muttered to me.

"I heard that!" said Fitzgerald.

With Fitzgerald's prodding we got a nice fire going in a circle of rocks. For a while we sat there, staring into the warm flames. Fitzgerald opened a can of peas and we ate.

I was feeling pretty good, not worrying too much.

But then Olive growled a low language grunt that meant, roughly, "THE DEVIL!"

I scooted backward quickly.

"Sorry," she apologized. "It's just that we're so close! If only I had remembered to bring the maps! Then we could have used the Secret Way!"

She pushed away her peas and slumped down in a hump of gloom.

"I shouldn't have let you guys come in the first place," she grumbled. "And I should have remembered the maps. Now look what I've gotten you into!"

"No sense moaning over what can't be undone," said Fitzgerald. "Or trying to take blame on yourself for what others have decided to do either. The thing to do is, face facts and make a plan. We're not injured, and we have some supplies."

He looked around, taking stock of the situation. "So, what do you think? Should we make an attempt at the Mound, or hole up here for the winter, or walk overland back to the City of Ruins, or what?"

"Attempt the Mound!" I shouted.

"Hmpf," grunted Olive. "You don't know what you're saying. The Fog is deadly—*Once in, never out!* There's no way to get from here to the Mound, except by the Secret Way."

"So," I said. "What about the Secret Way?"

"What about it?" she snapped back at me. "We'll never find it."

"We can try," I said. "There's the Eagle Tree already. That was on the map, so we know we're in the right area. We just have to look for a Bear-shaped Rock and the Waterfall Entrance and—"

"What are you talking about, Thelonious?" demanded Fitzgerald.

"The Secret Way!" I said. "You saw the map. We all saw it!"

"I just glanced at it," Fitzgerald said.

"I saw it," said Olive slowly. "Now that you mention it, I remember the Eagle Tree was on there. But the other stuff, well, I can't say I remember much else."

She sat up a little straighter. "Do you remember it well, Thelonious? Could you draw it?"

I took a stick and made a few lines in the dirt.

"I don't remember it all," I apologized. "There was a place at the bottom called Bear Rock, and the Eagle Tree was over here.

"And there was the Mushroom Cave, about here, and then the Grotto, like so, and the Waterfall Entrance . . ."

"That's amazing, Thelonious!" Olive said. "How can you remember all that? And you only saw it once!"

"He's got a good memory," Fitzgerald said. "It probably comes from learning all those legends by heart."

"I don't remember all of it," I said modestly.

"Yes, and there's the problem," said Olive. "What if we start out, based on this drawing, and then we lose our way and end up in the fog?"

"Well," said Fitzgerald, "if we could just find the entrance, at least we'd have a place to shelter. I say we start searching for a rock that looks like a bear! How hard can that be?"

Warmed by the fire, Brown woke up and poked his head out of the backpack.

"Are we there yet?" he asked.

13

BWOO BWOO

145

150

THIS MUST BE **THE GROTTO.**

I NEVER EVEN KNEW THIS PLACE EXISTED.

COOL.

OLIVE, LOOK AT THE WATERFALL ON THE OTHER SIDE OF THE GROTTO.

ON THE MAP IT SAID SOMETHING ABOUT A **WATERFALL ENTRANCE.**

LET'S GO SEE IF WE CAN FIND IT!

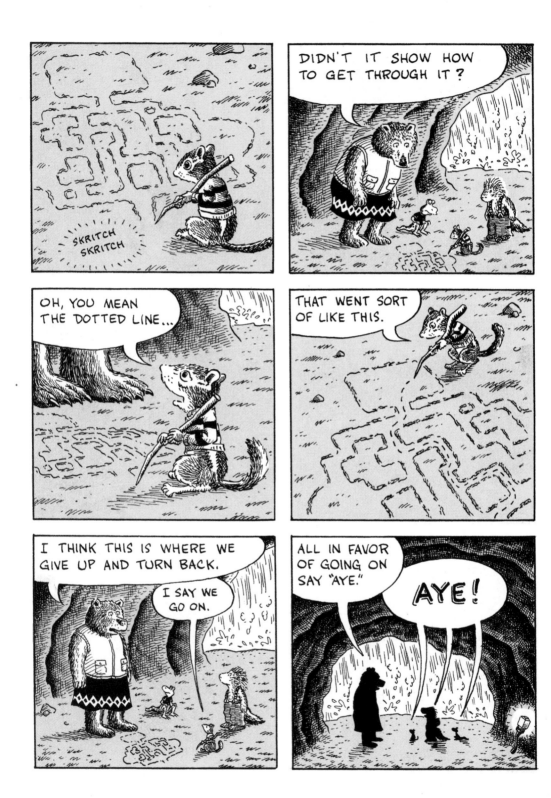

159

14

The Labyrinth

In the beginning, there was BWCC BWCC, and the great WCC MEH danced the FIRE OF LIFE!

That's it! I thought. Everything was suddenly clear to me—the meaning of life, the beginning of the world—everything! If only I could get rid of all that noise, so I could concentrate . . . and remember . . . *Go away. Let me alone. I must remember . . .*

"WAKE UP! Thelonious, wake up. Are you all right?"

It was that annoying lizard, Brown. He was leaning on my chest, yelling in my face, and slapping me on the cheeks.

"Get off!" I said, struggling to sit up.

I looked around. "Where is the great WOO MEH?" I said. "And the Fire of Life?"

"What Fire of Life?" said Brown.

I saw that we were still in the tunnel. Olive and Fitzgerald were sleeping.

"Huh?" I said to Brown.

"You just asked me about the Fire of Life," said Brown.

"I did?" An image was fading from my memory. I felt that it was important, but it was slipping away.

"Ooooooh," moaned Fitzgerald. "Stop the spinning."

He stood up, holding on to his head.

Olive opened her eyes. "What's that lovely smell?" she asked. "Caramels?"

"Peppermint," said Brown.

"What?" Olive said.

"Peppermint," Brown repeated. "The fog smells like peppermint."

"The Fog! What do you mean?" Olive struggled to her feet, looked wildly around, and sniffed the air. "Where are we? How do you know what the fog smells like?"

"Relax," said Brown. "We're out of it now."

"Out of it *now?*" cried Olive. "You mean we were in it!"

"Didn't you say, Olive, that the fog is supposed to make you act crazy? So that you don't know what you're doing, and you go farther and farther into it, and then you can never get out?"

"That's right. That's what they told me," Olive agreed.

"Well, we went into a tunnel, and you three started acting crazy. Then I noticed the peppermint smell. It was damp and misty, too, now that I think about it. You guys wouldn't listen to reason. I had to trick you into following me back out. And then you all passed out. It's that tunnel over there," he said, pointing. "See, I put an *X* in front of it so we won't go that way again."

"I don't believe we were in the fog at all," said Olive. "*Once in, never out,* that's what the warning says, so how could we have gone in, and come out again?"

"Well," said Fitzgerald, "somebody, sometime, must have come out. How else would you even know it was there? And what its effect was like?"

"Don't you remember 'BWOO BWOO'?" asked Brown.

"BWOO BWOO!" I shouted, jumping up. "That's it!"

"That's what?" Fitzgerald asked.

"I don't remember." I sat down again. "It seemed important at the time."

Brown told us exactly what had happened, and I thought it must be true. I could almost remember it.

"Well, it makes sense that the Secret Way shouldn't be too easy," Fitzgerald said. "I guess some of the Labyrinth tunnels lead directly into the fog."

"They do!" I remembered it now. "On the map there were a few circles marked 'FOG PIT!'" I told the others.

"*Now* you tell us!" Fitzgerald said.

"If we were in the fog, why didn't it make *you* crazy?" Olive asked Brown.

"I don't know," Brown said. "It must be a mammal thing."

"You mean reptiles aren't affected by the fog?" Olive looked thoughtful. "That could be. There aren't any reptiles on the Mound, you know."

"No reptiles?" Brown asked.

"I don't think they like northern climates," Fitzgerald said.

I looked at the tunnel that was marked with an *X*. "How do we know we won't come to a Fog Pit in another tunnel?" I asked.

"I've been thinking about that," Brown said. "I thought I could go first, and if it doesn't smell like peppermint, then I'll call you and you can follow me."

I must say, I thought that was pretty brave.

Fitzgerald said, "How will you see, Brown? The torch is too big for you."

Olive picked up the torch and studied the glowing rock. "Maybe I can chip

off a piece of it," she said.

She knocked at a corner of it with
a piece of rock from the ground. But
instead of breaking the torch, the
piece of rock from the ground got
smashed to bits.

"Hmmm, it looks like this torch is

made out of a very hard substance," she said. "It would probably take some-

thing like a diamond to cut it."

Brown said, "I've got a diamond."

Olive looked at him. "Excuse me, Brown. Did you just say you have a

diamond?"

For an answer, Brown rummaged around under his shirt. I remembered

how when I first met him he had talked about some gems he had gotten from

the Dragon Lady. I thought I would like to know what else he had under

there, but he turned away and I couldn't see.

He handed the diamond to Olive, who held it up next to the torch. It

reflected the light in a million tiny stars.

"No," she said, trying to give the diamond back to Brown. "It's too beau-

tiful. I don't know what will happen to it."

Brown wouldn't take it.

"Go ahead," he said. "It's only a stone."

I was surprised to hear him say that. I remembered how much he loved his precious gems.

Olive studied Brown's face.

"Go ahead," he repeated. "It won't do me much good if we never get out of here."

Olive sighed and put the diamond against the glowing stone light. "I guess you're right," she said. "Maybe I can just score it."

She sliced the diamond across a corner of the light. It made a tiny line. Then she tapped it with the diamond and a small glowing chunk broke neatly off and rolled to Brown's feet.

He picked it up and held it on the flat of his palm. Olive set the diamond beside it.

The two stones lit up Brown's scaly chin. He smiled, kissed the diamond, and slipped it back inside his shirt.

"Let's go, then," he said, and started bravely off down an unmarked tunnel.

"Don't follow too close," he said. "I'll call you if it's okay, and I'll come back if I smell *anything*, peppermint or otherwise."

We followed at a safe distance behind Brown's tiny light. Each tunnel led to more entrances to other tunnels. It was all very confusing.

Luckily Fitzgerald was dragging the stick to mark where we had been.

Twice Brown hurried back and made us turn around. Then Fitzgerald would put an X by that tunnel entrance, and we would try another.

Sometimes Brown would come to a dead end. Then Fitzgerald would put an O by the entrance.

After a while we stopped to eat.

We didn't talk much.

After eating we slept for a few hours. Nobody knew what time it was, or how long we'd been in there.

Then we began again.

If Fitzgerald hadn't been marking our trail, we could have been going around in circles and not even known it! And if Brown hadn't been scouting ahead, we probably would have been in the bottom of a Fog Pit.

Nobody asked me about the map anymore.

Up ahead I could see Brown's light getting bigger. He was coming back.

"I found something!" he called. "It's another dead end, but there's a little cave with a capsule in it, and it says 'FROZEN SCIENTIST' on the front."

"I don't think that was on the map," I said.

We followed Brown back down the tunnel, and there was the capsule just like he said.

Olive held up the big torch.

"FROZEN SCIENTIST," I read. Of course, Brown had already told us what it said.

There were more words underneath. "P-U-S-H . . . R-E-D . . . ," I began reading carefully.

"'Push red button to activate thawing process,'" Brown read.

Show-off.

"Well," I said, when nobody moved, "shouldn't we push it?"

"WAIT!" said Fitzgerald. "Do you know anything about this, Olive?"

"No," she said. "But that doesn't mean much. I wasn't told about the Secret Way at all, remember. Or the Grotto, or anything."

"Are any of the Fog Mound animals scientists?" Fitzgerald asked her.

"No. I think it was a scientist who built the Mound, though. A human scientist, during the Occupation."

"Aha!" said Fitzgerald. "A human! Well, we don't want any humans, thank you. Look what they did the last time they were here!"

"I thought you didn't know what they did," I said.

Fitzgerald glared at me. "I don't know *exactly* what they did," he admitted. "But everybody knows they practically destroyed the whole planet and every living thing on it!"

"I think the planet is doing pretty well," I said, thinking of all the tall nut-bearing trees in the Untamed Forest. "Anyway, if there's a human in there, I want to see it."

Olive wiped the little glass window and looked in. "It looks empty," she said. "Except for an old rag in the corner."

"Why would you want to thaw out an old rag?" I said.

"Let's see," said Brown. "Open the door."

"Not so fast." Fitzgerald moved in front of the door with his quills slightly raised.

Brown and I backed up.

"You can't trust humans," Fitzgerald said. "It might be an illusion that it's empty. We could be unleashing a monster!"

"I say we push the button," I said. "That's what it says to do."

"I say we just open the door and have a look," Brown said. "Didn't Olive say it was empty? Somebody must have thawed the scientist a long time ago. Bears have been coming through here for generations, haven't they, Olive?"

"Yes, they have. But they might not have come this way. I mean, if they already knew the correct route, they wouldn't have any reason to come down this particular tunnel, would they?

"I think the scientist who built the Fog Mound was a good human," she added slowly, "and we should follow his directions."

Fitzgerald frowned and folded his arms, but he stepped away from the capsule.

Olive looked at me and Brown. We both nodded. She pushed the button.

Nothing happened.

Olive shrugged and looked in the little window again.

"Look!" Brown said suddenly, pointing.

There, below the sign about pushing the button, a bar of red light was showing. And below that, in red letters, a new sign said, NOW THAWING. We watched the bar of red light fill in.

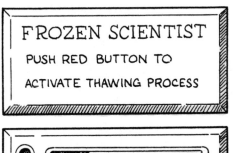

BLIP, it extended to the right. *BLIP, BLIP, BLIP, BLIP* it went all the way across and stopped. The NOW THAWING sign went off.

We stared at it, waiting.

Then white letters flashed on and off.

THAWING COMPLETE. THAWING COMPLETE.

There was a little click, and the door to the capsule swung slowly open.

We all crowded around and looked in.

Like Olive said, it was empty, except for the old white rag in the corner.

Then the rag moved!

"Yah!" I jumped behind Fitzgerald.

The rag was thrashing all around.

Olive reached in, hooked it with a claw, and lifted it up.

15

The Frozen Scientist

177

16

The Fog Mound

"Mother!" Olive cried.
"Oh, Olive, my good girl!
You've come home to us!" A
short, round bear jumped up
and wrapped her arms
around Olive's broad middle.

A young bear peeked in the doorway, shrieked, and ran out again, shouting, "Olive's back!"

More bears arrived, including Olive's father, the biggest one of all.

"Here's Pubba!" someone said, and the clamor of welcoming voices died down.

"So, Olive," he snarled. "You finally decided to come home. I'm sure that makes your mother very happy, but you've got a lot of explaining to do."

I decided to hide under the table for safety.

Olive didn't look worried. She laughed, squeezed Pubba's huge arm, and said, "I've got so much to tell you!"

From my spot under the table I watched as more animals arrived—rabbits, squirrels, mice, even some other chipmunks and a pair of porcupines like Fitzgerald, and otters, chickens, raccoons, and skunks. A donkey stuck its head in the window, and a duck waddled past my hiding spot.

I also saw a smiling cat and a sleek fox.

The other animals were not afraid of them. In fact, I saw one mouse speak to the cat and another actually leaned against her side.

Still, I was glad I was behind the table leg where no one could see me.

Olive was describing the City of Ruins. "I met some wonderful animals there," she said. "And I even brought some home with me!"

She looked around for us. "Where are you?"

Fitzgerald stepped forward.

"Oh, there you are. This is Fitzgerald Porcupine, who lives in a bookstore in the City of Ruins. He has even more books than we do!"

Fitzgerald mumbled something and looked at the floor.

"And where's Thelonious?" said Olive.

I peeked out and squeaked, "Here, Olive."

She offered me a paw, so I let her lift me up onto the table.

"This little chipmunk from the Untamed Forest made it possible for us to find the Secret Way!" she announced.

"And of course, Brown Lizard got us through the labyrinth!"

Brown climbed up to join me. He gave a little bow.

The other animals stared. Olive had said there were no reptiles on the Fog Mound, so I guess he looked strange to them.

Olive began telling about the ratminks.

Somebody set a bowl of honeyed nuts beside me. Yum.

More food appeared—breads, fruits, seeds, and Olive's favorite caramels (which were good, but sticky), and more.

Olive was telling everyone about how I could remember the map even when nobody else could.

I liked hearing it. I liked the heavy, warm feeling of having a full tummy. I liked the shiny eyes and interested faces all around me.

I heard Olive say, "Then Brown came running back to us saying, 'There's a capsule with a sign on it that says FROZEN SCIENTIST'—" But she stopped short, looked from me to Brown to Fitzgerald and said, "Where's Bill!"

"Bill?" asked Olive's father. "Who's Bill?"

"Bill is the frozen scientist!" said Olive. "I was just going to tell you about him, Pubba. He's a very small human. We think he must have shrunk in the freezing chamber. We thawed him out, and he led us to the Works, but now we've lost him!"

"A human?" Pubba was aghast! "Did you say a human?"

I said to Olive, "I know he came through the secret door. I saw him in the Works."

"Me too," said Brown. "He was looking at the machinery."

Fitzgerald said, "Did anybody see him after that?"

"No."

"Uh-uh."

"Not me."

Brown and I jumped down from the table.

Olive said, "The rest of you better wait here. We don't want to frighten him."

We hurried back through the big rooms toward the Works.

The other animals waited in the kitchen. All except Pubba, who rushed ahead with Olive.

"But, Olive," I heard him saying. "A human? Are you sure? Do you think it's *our* scientist? The Fog Mound scientist? What's he doing in the Works? Do you think he's safe?"

"I don't know, Pubba," she replied. "He doesn't speak."

The Works were in a series of huge rooms under Cliff House. The big machines were humming along, bringing water, regulating temperature, even (as I learned later) making the fog!

"Bill?" Olive called.

"What if he's gumming up the Works?" boomed Pubba in his big, growly voice.

"Don't scare him," said Olive.

I ran around the floor, looking under everything. After all, Bill was small like me. But Brown crawled up the wall so he could get a bird's-eye view, and it was Brown who found him.

"There he is!" Brown called, pointing.

Bill was sitting cross-legged on top of a big tank. He was smiling at a lit-up panel of dials and knobs and bar graphs and switches.

"He went right for the controls!" whispered Pubba. "But at least he isn't touching anything.

"Are you sure he's alive?" he added. "He looks just like the old Buddha in the garden."

(Later we saw the Buddha statue in the garden, and I could see what Pubba meant. They both had the same goofy smile on their faces.)

Bill came quietly. He didn't look frightened at all. He laughed when Pubba offered him a ride on his paw, and climbed right up as if he had been riding on bear paws all his life. He seemed to be especially interested in Pubba's big thumb.

But he didn't answer any of Pubba's questions.

Back on the kitchen table Bill picked up a grape, sniffed it, laughed at it, and started nibbling.

All the animals stared at him, and he beamed back at them.

After a minute or two I walked carefully around the edge of the room until I was next to Olive's mother. I touched her arm, and she smiled at me, so I whispered in her ear.

She nodded and got to her feet. She went to a drawer, opened it, took out a small cloth, and offered it to Bill.

Bill took it and wrapped it around himself. Now I felt better. It didn't seem right—all that bare skin. Human beings were *meant* to wear clothes.

That night we slept on a human bed in Cliff House.

The next morning a young female chipmunk woke us up.

"Get up, get up, lazy newcomers!" she sang from the bedpost. "Olive says I can show you all around the Fog Mound."

But first there was breakfast.

I watched Olive's mother make it. She put cow's milk and shelled eggs and ground wheat flour in a bowl and mixed them all up. Then she dropped blobs of the stuff on a hot pan and turned them over so they were browned on both sides. She called them pancakes. Olive put berries and maple syrup on top of the pancakes and we ate them, and they were delicious!

Our chipmunk guide was called Cluid.

She skipped ahead of us and beckoned, saying, "Come this way please. We'll be starting in the Cliff House flower gardens. All of these flowers have been here since the beginning. They were planted by humans!"

It was all a big wild, luscious tangle of leaves and flowers. There were pathways laid out in flat stones for bears, and lots of low tunnels running under the bushes. The heavy blossoms glowed in shades of red and gold,

and some of the leaves were turning their fall colors. It was very pretty.

There were low walls made out of stones, and stone benches where you could have a picnic; there were stone bowls that filled with water when it rained; and there was the Buddha statue, smiling like Bill.

"Do you notice how it's still warm here?" said Brown. "Outside the Mound it was almost too cold for me!"

"Almost?" I snorted. "You were a basket case!"

"That's because of the Works," Cluid explained. "They control the hot springs, and the fog. They keep it warmer here than in the surrounding mountains. That extends the growing season and makes it more comfortable for us too."

"C'mon!" She leaped ahead, eager to show us everything.

We came to some long houses made out of glass.

Cluid led us in through a small door. "This is where the food plants begin," she said.

"Aha!" said Fitzgerald. "Greenhouses!"

It was very warm and moist inside and full of green, growing plants. I guess that's why they were called greenhouses.

Small animals were working on rows of tiny seedlings, carefully pinching them back and thinning them out. They told us that the seedlings would grow all winter in the warm glass houses and be ready for planting outside in the spring.

"Everyone on the Mound does their part to help the others," Cluid explained. "That's important in a community like this."

Brown liked the warmth in the greenhouses.

"This is great!" he said. "I could be happy working in here." But the small animals looked away shyly.

Then there was the cow barn, empty now because the cows were all out in the field. It was dark in the barn, and it smelled nice.

Next, we went to see the cows themselves.

They seemed to have a happy life, eating in the field, sleeping in the big barn, and providing milk.

"We can produce a lot of extra milk," said one of the cows to me. "And we're happy to do our share. In exchange, the bears plant and cut hay for us."

I was beginning to get the idea.

There was another big barn full of huge wagons and machines that go— like spreaders and reapers.

"Olive works here," said Cluid. "She's good with engines."

I nodded. "We know," I said.

Fitzgerald was interested in the agricultural operations. He said that the whole setup of the place reminded him of a medieval castle.

"It's like King Arthur's time," he said. "Do you know any of the legends about King Arthur, Thelonious? About the Knights of the Round Table and Sir Lancelot and Merlin?"

"I know one about Merlin, the magician who changes a human boy into different animals," I said. "I didn't think it was true, though."

"That's the one!" Fitzgerald said. "That boy grows up to be King Arthur. The story isn't true. Ha, ha! How could a human get changed into an animal? But there really were medieval castles, with moats around them, sort of like the circle of fog here. And they grew their own food and the animals contributed eggs and milk and . . ."

He looked uncomfortable and changed the subject.

"Where to next, Cluid?" he said.

Cluid took us to Burrowtown and we met her family.

Cluid said, "You can call us Small or Chipmunk, either one. Sometimes it's more convenient to refer to all the Smalls together. You could be called Small too, Thelonious."

I wasn't sure I would like that. I was a Chipmunk and proud of it.

In Burrowtown they had their own Works and their own storerooms, with underground tunnels leading directly to the Cliff House basements.

There were even some Small businesses, including a tailoring and knitting

shop. I ordered a new sweater, and they measured Bill for trousers and a new white coat. Fitzgerald was too big and had to wait outside.

We had lunch with Cluid's family—seed sandwiches.

Then we went to an area called Fernland—a beautiful place of tall trees, moss banks, fern groves, and a flowing brook.

We followed the brook to Turtle Pond, and then we walked back on a hard-packed dirt road, passing the vegetable gardens and the chicken houses and several human buildings made of stone, coming at last to YASA—the "Young and Smalls Apartments."

And there was Olive, waiting for us.

"Did you love it?" she called before we were even up to her. "I wish I could have taken you around myself this first time, but I knew you'd be curious to see everything right away, and Mother and Pubba wanted me. They're planning a big welcome home party for us! It's tomorrow night. There'll be music and dancing and lots of food, and you'll get to meet everyone."

Olive took us inside YASA.

It's an old human building that has been made over for small animals, but the main entrance area is still big enough for Olive and Fitz. It's made out of stone and set right into the hillside below Cliff House, with a view over the fog to the distant mountains.

"It's nice, isn't it?" Cluid said. "I live here, you know, and there's an empty apartment on the third floor. We were hoping that you and Brown and Bill would like to move in. Do you want to see it? There's an elevator. And electricity and running water. We have a group kitchen and a gathering area, but you can cook in your own apartment too."

Of course we wanted to see it.

Olive took Fitzgerald back up to Cliff House, and we went to look at the apartment.

The first thing I noticed was that somebody had put out some food for us.

Brown said, "We'll take it!"

We ate at a dining table in front of the window, watching the sun set over the mountains. Bill fell asleep at the table, and Cluid left us to return to her own apartment.

I walked around, switching on the electric lights and checking out the sleeping areas.

"This is a pretty cool place, huh, Brown?" I said. I switched a light off and on again.

Brown was busy pulling out a pouch from under his shirt.

"Uh, I've got something for you," he said.

He handed me a small bundle wrapped in colored paper.

"For me?"

I unwrapped it quickly.

It was a smooth rock. A rock of rainbow colors! It was the most beautiful thing I had ever seen! All sparkly colors coming from within, like magic. I looked from the beautiful rock to Brown in amazement.

"I heard you talking," he explained. "I heard you say you wanted a rock of rainbow colors. It's a black opal."

"It's a jewel, isn't it?" I said. I shook my head. "No, it's too good."

"No, it's not," he said.

"Yes, it is. Why should you give me a present anyway? I haven't got anything for you."

"So what are you saying? You don't want it? Okay, give it back. We'll forget I ever gave it to you." He held out his hand.

I grabbed my rock of rainbow colors to my chest. My opal.

"Look," he said. "If it wasn't for you, I'd still be a slave in the City of Ruins. And I was going to trade you to the Dragon Lady for a ruby. So, I'm sorry, see? It's a peace offering. Do you want it, or not?"

"I want it," I said. "I want it a lot. Thanks, Brown. But I wish I had a present for you. I haven't always been nice to you, and you saved us from the fog, and . . ."

"Oh, shut up," said Brown. "Go to sleep."

I slipped my opal into my bedding.

"Brown?" I said.

He grunted.

"Are you excited about the big welcome party tomorrow night?"

There was no reply.

Brown was fast asleep.

17

Party

204

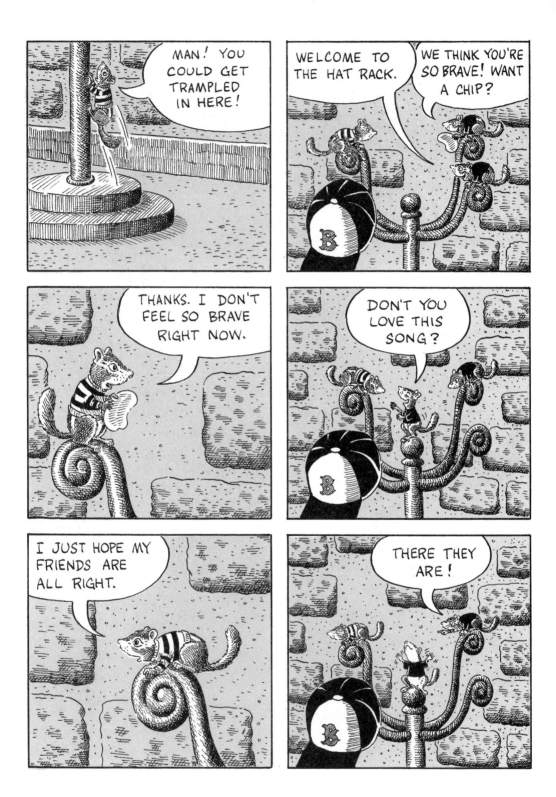

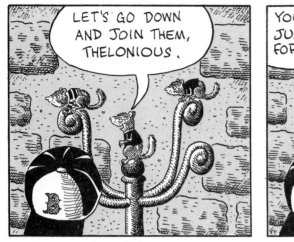

211

IT'S BEAUTIFUL HERE.

THERE'S NO PLACE LIKE IT ON EARTH.

ARE YOU SURE ABOUT THAT, OLIVE? SOMETIMES I WONDER.

WHAT DO YOU MEAN, AUNT ELF?

WELL, THINK ABOUT THE END OF THE HUMAN OCCUPATION. THE ENVIRONMENT IS POISONED. THE ICE CAPS ARE MELTING. SCIENTISTS ALL OVER THE WORLD ARE LOOKING FOR SOLUTIONS. SUPPOSE BILL WAS A SCIENTIST WHO SAW WHAT WAS COMING.

BILL DECIDES TO SET UP A SAFE COMMUNITY FOR ANIMALS. HE MAKES THE WORKS. HE GATHERS THE ANIMALS. HE FREEZES HIMSELF. WHO'S TO SAY SOME OTHER SCIENTIST SOMEWHERE DOESN'T HAVE A SIMILAR IDEA?

IF ONLY BILL COULD TALK! JUST THINK WHAT HE COULD TELL US.

F...F...